How many *Fairy Animals* books have you collected?

- Chloe the Kitten
- Bella the Bunny
- Paddy the Puppy
- Mia the Mouse
- Poppy the Pony
- Hailey the Hedgehog
- Sophie the Squirrel
- Daisy the Deer
- Kylie the Kitten
- Paige the Pony
- Penny the Puppy
- Bailey the Bunny

Fairy Animals

of Misty Wood

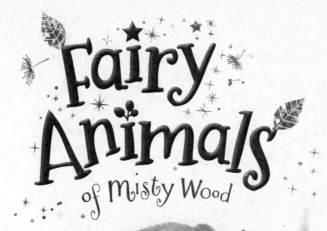

Penny the Puppy

Lily Small

Henry Holt and Company
New York

With special thanks to Anne Marie Ryan.

Henry Holt and Company, *Publishers since 1866*
Henry Holt® is a registered trademark of Macmillan Publishing Group, LLC.
175 Fifth Avenue, New York, NY 10010
mackids.com

First published in the United States in 2018 by Henry Holt and Company.
Originally published in Great Britain in 2015 by Egmont UK Limited.

Library of Congress Control Number: 2017945046
ISBN: 978-1-250-29721-1

Our books may be purchased in bulk for promotional, educational, or business use.
Please contact your local bookseller or the Macmillan Corporate
and Premium Sales Department at (800) 221-7945 ext. 5442
or by e-mail at MacmillanSpecialMarkets@macmillan.com.

First American edition, 2018
Printed in the United States of America
by LSC Communications, Harrisonburg, Virginia

1 3 5 7 9 10 8 6 4 2

Contents

CHAPTER ONE

School Bells

Penny the Puppy *loved* going to school. She loved playing with her friends. She loved her teacher, Miss Pammy. And she loved learning how

to be a good little Pollen Puppy.

There was just one problem. The Fairy Animals of Misty Wood went to school outdoors. And on sunny spring mornings, there was no place in the world more glorious than Misty Wood.

There were flowers blooming all around, trees rustling in the breeze, and the sky was always a brilliant shade of sapphire blue. There were so many beautiful things to gaze

at that it was hard for Penny to concentrate on her lessons!

Today, the young Pollen Puppies were having a lesson in Bluebell Glade. Penny looked around at the carpet of violet blossoms swaying in the warm breeze. She sniffed deeply as their sweet perfume wafted over her, blending with the fresh, earthy smell of Misty Wood. *Mmm*—it was lovely!

Penny closed her big chocolaty-brown eyes for a moment. She imagined herself rolling around and around in the flowers, until her golden fur was covered in their scent.

A gentle voice interrupted her daydream. "Didn't you get enough sleep last night, Penny?"

Penny's eyes flew open wide. *Oops!* Her teacher had caught her daydreaming again.

"N-no, miss," said Penny. "I mean, yes." She sighed dreamily and tried to explain. "It's just that the bluebells are so pretty and sweet smelling. I was wondering what it would be like to roll around in them."

"The bluebells are beautiful, Penny," Miss Pammy said kindly. "But today's lesson is very important, so please pay attention."

Then Miss Pammy turned back to the rest of the class. "As you know,

all the fairy animals in Misty Wood have important jobs to do," she said. "We are Pollen Puppies, so we flick our tails to send pollen into the air. Can anyone tell me why?"

Penny's friend Perry, a perky little puppy with brown and white patches, flapped his sparkling wings frantically. "To make more flowers grow!" he answered.

Miss Pammy smiled. "That's correct, Perry."

Penny sighed. She wished she could be clever like Perry. He never seemed to get distracted.

"But it's important to flick only *five* flowers at a time," Miss Pammy said. "Otherwise you will fill the air with too much pollen." Gazing around at the eager puppies, she asked, "Does anyone know why we don't want too much pollen in the air?"

Once again, Perry knew

the answer. He bounced up and down, wagging his tail furiously until Miss Pammy called on him. "Because it will make other fairy animals sneeze, miss!" he said.

Fluttering over to a cluster of bluebells, Miss Pammy showed the class what to do.

Everyone counted along as she wagged her fluffy tail over five stems of bluebells. Every time her tail swished over a flower, a little

cloud of pollen floated into the air.

"Now it's your turn," Miss Pammy told the class. "I want you to spread out and practice counting to five."

Bluebell Glade was suddenly filled with a flurry of sparkling wings. They glittered like jewels in the sunlight as Pollen Puppies flew around, looking for a good spot to practice counting.

Penny landed softly among a cluster of bluebells. Nearby, Perry was already hard at work. His brown tail flicked back and forth over the flowers as he loudly counted to five.

Determined to show her teacher that she had been paying attention, Penny brushed her tail over one flower.

"ONE," she said loudly as a puff of pollen rose into the air.

"TWO," she said, carefully wagging her tail over another graceful stem of bluebells.

"THREE," she said, sweeping her tail over a third stem.

Penny took a deep breath,

enjoying the delicious scent of the bluebells. Then she shook her head and forced herself to concentrate. She didn't want to make a mistake.

What comes after three? she asked herself.

As she tried to remember, Penny peered down at the delicate bluish-purple flower by her paws. With their curling petals, the dainty blossoms really did look like tiny bells.

13

Her ears pricked up with curiosity. Penny wondered what bluebells would sound like if they could make music. She was sure it would be a sweet, chiming sound. Suddenly, Penny imagined a tune played by hundreds of bluebells tinkling on the breeze.

The song was so lively that Penny couldn't resist dancing. Fluttering her glittering wings and swishing her tail back and forth to

14

the rhythm, Penny danced around Bluebell Glade to the imaginary sound of a bluebell band.

"La, di-da, la-la," she sang happily, under her breath. *"La-la-la—"*

Suddenly, a very loud noise interrupted the music in Penny's head.

"Ahhhhhh-CHOOOOO!"

It was Chloe the Cobweb Kitten, flying back from her morning duty of decorating cobwebs with sparkling

15

dewdrops. Her pretty eyes were streaming, and her pink nose twitched as she sneezed again and again.

Penny looked up in dismay. All around her was a huge cloud of pollen, drifting into the sky. She'd lost count of how many bluebells she was flicking!

"I'm so sorry!" Penny called to Chloe. But the Cobweb Kitten couldn't reply. She sneezed and

spluttered as she tried to get away

from the pollen.

Miss Pammy hurried over.

"Penny! How many bluebells did

you flick?"

17

Penny hung her head. "I'm not sure, miss. I counted to three, but then I started thinking about bluebells making music and . . . er . . . I lost count."

"It's lovely that you have such a big imagination, Penny." Miss Pammy sighed. "But being a Pollen Puppy is a very important job. And to do it properly, you need to be able to count."

"I'm sorry, miss," Penny said

sadly, her eyes brimming with tears.

"Let's try again," her teacher said gently. "You said you flicked three bluebells. So if you flicked two more, how many bluebells would that make altogether?"

"Er . . . four?" Penny guessed.

Miss Pammy shook her head sadly. "No, dear."

Perry bounded over. "The answer's five!" he barked.

As usual, Perry was right.

"I'm never going to be a good Pollen Puppy," Penny whimpered, her pink wings drooping.

Her teacher patted her with a soft paw. "Of course you will," she said. "You just need to concentrate harder on your schoolwork, and practice your counting. Can you try that for me?"

Penny's wings perked up again. "I will," she promised, nodding so hard that her ears flapped. "I'm

going to learn how to count to five *today*, and by tomorrow I'll be perfect at it!"

Penny was determined to be a good Pollen Puppy and make Miss Pammy proud. She would learn how to count to five—even if it meant never daydreaming again!

CHAPTER TWO

Tea for Two

For the rest of the lesson, Penny
listened carefully as her teacher
explained how to tell when bluebells
were ready to make pollen. Her

attention didn't wander once, even when a nearby bird chirped a beautiful song. Nor when she saw a pretty blue beetle scuttle by, so shiny that it looked like a precious gem.

Before long, Miss Pammy announced that it was time to go home. The frisky Pollen Puppies yipped joyfully and frolicked around Bluebell Glade.

"Remember," Miss Pammy

called after the playful puppies,
"only five flowers at a time!"

Perry dashed over to Penny.
"We're going to play sliding down
the rainbow," he said, wagging his
tail excitedly. "Want to come?"

"I can't," Penny answered
reluctantly. "I need to learn how
to count."

Penny *loved* sliding down the
rainbow with her friends. It was one
of her favorite things to do. But she

had promised Miss Pammy that she
would practice counting.

"You can count the colors of
the rainbow," Perry suggested. He
pointed a paw at the enormous
rainbow that shone in the sky above
Misty Wood. "It's easy—there are
seven colors." Then Perry rattled
them off. "Red, orange, yellow,
green, blue, indigo, and violet!"

Penny tried to count the
beautiful bands of color sparkling

in the sunlight. "One . . . two . . .
three," she counted slowly.

But before she'd even counted
half the colors, she was picturing
herself whooshing down the
rainbow at top speed.

"I'm sorry, Perry," she said
sadly. "Rainbows are just too much
fun. I need to find something really
boring to count."

"Okay," Perry said. "Good
luck!" Waving good-bye with his

paw, he flew into the air and caught up with a group of Pollen Puppies heading toward the rainbow slide.

Penny heaved a sigh. She wished she could join her friends. But she wished even more that she could be a good Pollen Puppy—and to do that, she needed to know how to count to five.

Fluttering her wings, Penny rose into the sky. Below her, Misty

Wood spread out in a sea of color. Beyond the violet carpet of Bluebell Glade, Dandelion Dell glowed with hundreds of golden dandelions bobbing in the sunshine.

The silvery waters of Moonshine Pond sparkled invitingly and Honeydew Meadow was a vibrant emerald green, dotted with white daisies. In the very heart of Misty Wood was a cluster of ancient trees. Penny decided to head there first.

★

Penny landed in a clearing surrounded by mighty oak trees. Their glossy green leaves rustled in the breeze. She thought it sounded like they were whispering. *What secrets could the oak trees be telling one another?* she wondered.

Maybe they're talking about the secret to becoming so tall, she thought, smiling, *or how to grow so many leaves.*

But then she caught herself

starting to daydream and shook
her head sternly. *Focus, Penny!*

Penny put her little nose to
the ground and started sniffing.
She padded around the clearing,

32

looking for something boring to count. It wasn't easy, as everything in Misty Wood was so interesting!

At the base of a tall tree with a gnarled trunk, Penny found a hollow lined with soft moss. She felt around inside it with her paw and discovered a stash of acorns.

Acorns aren't very interesting, thought Penny. *They're perfect for practicing counting.*

Taking a deep breath, Penny

began to count. She picked the acorns up one at a time and carefully lined them in a row. "One . . . two . . ."

But when Penny picked up the third acorn, its cap fell off. Holding the little cap in her paw, Penny peered at it closely.

It looks like a hat made for a teeny tiny elf, she thought with a giggle. She turned it over. Now it looked like a dainty little cup.

Penny suddenly imagined herself at a tea party. All the guests were fairy animals, looking their very best! Their wings glittered, their fur gleamed, and beautiful flower garlands sparkled around their necks.

"Do have some rosehip tea, dear," Penny said, pretending to be a host offering tea to her guests.

"Why, thank you," Penny replied in her poshest voice. "How

kind of you to offer, Madame Rosehip Blossom." She lifted the tiny acorn cap to her mouth and pretended to sip from it. She could practically taste the sweet rosehip tea.

"My name isn't Madame Rosehip Blossom," someone said crossly, making Penny jump. "And I *didn't* offer you my acorns."

Penny swirled around and saw a Stardust Squirrel staring at her suspiciously.

"Oh, no, I wasn't eating your acorns," Penny explained. "I was just pretending to drink from them." She showed him the acorn cap. "See? It looks like a cute little cup."

The Stardust Squirrel squinted at the acorn cap. "Oh. They *do* look like little cups!" He smiled at Penny. "My name's Sammy, by the way."

"I'm Penny. Do you want to have a fairy tea party with me?" Penny asked her new friend. Sammy nodded eagerly.

"That can

be our table," Penny said, pointing to an old tree stump. "Let's make it look pretty enough for a fairy party!"

Sammy set the tree stump table with acorn caps. Penny picked a small bunch of violets and arranged them in the middle.

"It looks lovely," Penny said happily.

"Wait, something's missing," Sammy said. He twirled around,

giving his tail a shake, and suddenly the whole table was sparkling. The Stardust Squirrels' special job was to sprinkle Misty Wood with stardust from their big bushy tails. Now the clearing looked even more beautiful!

"I'll be Madame Rosehip Blossom," Penny said, picking up a twig and pretending it was a magic wand. "Can I offer you some delicious rosehip tea?"

Sammy giggled. "If it's all right with you, Madame Rosehip Blossom, I'd rather *eat* the acorns!"

So Sammy munched on acorns, while Penny sipped cup after cup of pretend rosehip tea.

"What lovely weather we've been having," Penny said, glancing at the sunlight streaming through the branches overhead. She hoped this was the sort of thing you talked about at tea parties.

Sammy just nodded. His cheeks were too full of nuts to speak!

Suddenly, a voice from up in a tree called out, "Sammy! Where are you?"

Sammy sprang to his feet.

"Oh no! My mom told me to bring five acorns home for lunch. I've got to go! It's been really fun playing with you, Penny—let's play again soon."

Sammy waved good-bye to Penny, and then quickly gathered up five acorns. He scampered up a nearby tree, leaving a trail of shimmering stardust behind him.

When Penny heard Sammy say *five*, she suddenly remembered

what she'd come into the woods
to do.

"Oh, dear," she said,
looking around the clearing. She
was *supposed* to be practicing
counting—not having a fairy tea
party with a new friend! Who knew
that acorns were so interesting?

The warm sun was shining
high above Misty Wood, so
there was still plenty of time to
find something else to count.

44

Something really boring, that
wouldn't make her want to
daydream or play. Penny just
needed to find it!

CHAPTER THREE

Princess Penny

Penny fluttered her wings and flew high into the air. As she left the trees behind, her big brown eyes scanned the ground,

searching for something to count.

Far below, Honeydew Meadow rippled in the breeze like a sea of green. But what were all those little white spots?

Penny let out a yelp of excitement. Daisies! There were lots and lots of them, so they'd be just right for counting practice.

She landed in the meadow and bounded around, picking daisies until she had a big bunch.

Right, she thought firmly. *This time I won't let anything distract me!*

"One," she said, picking up a daisy and setting it aside. "Two," she counted, carefully placing a second daisy next to the first one.

"Three," she said, putting another flower in the row.

I'm counting! Penny thought proudly. She stopped for a moment to admire how pretty the flowers looked, lined up in a row.

Penny thought that the daisies' snowy-white petals looked like little crowns around their yellow heads. And that gave Penny a brilliant idea. Daisies weren't just good for counting—they were also perfect for making crowns!

Penny picked up two daisies and wove their delicate stems together. Then she added another, and another, until she had a long chain of daisies. She joined the

two ends together to make a circle
and placed the crown on top of her
head.

Penny stood on her hind legs
and pranced around the meadow.
"I am Princess Penny, ruler of
Honeydew Meadow!" she barked
at the flowers around her. "I am
in charge of everyone, and you all
have to do whatever I say!"

"Oh, no, I don't," said a soft
voice.

Startled, Penny dropped down on all fours and spun around to see a silvery Bud Bunny. The bunny's soft whiskers trembled as she stared at Penny.

"Oh, hello," Penny said, hoping she hadn't upset the bunny. "I'm Penny. I was just playing at being a princess. I was trying to

boss around the daisies, not you!"

The Bud Bunny giggled, making her fluffy tail shake. *"Phew!"* she said. "Can I play, too?"

Penny wagged her tail in delight. Games were always much more fun if you had a friend to play with. "Of course! What's your name?" she asked the Bud Bunny.

"Bella," the bunny replied.

"Come on, then, Princess

Bella," Penny said. "We need to
make you a crown!"

Penny and Bella dashed around
the meadow, picking more daisies.
Whenever they came across a

flower that hadn't opened yet, Bella nudged the bud with her velvety nose and the petals unfurled as if by magic.

It was the Bud Bunnies' job to make flowers blossom, and Penny loved watching it happen.

When they'd gathered big bunches of daisies, Penny and Bella sat down in the sunshine and wove the stems together with their paws. But they didn't stop when they'd

finished making Bella's crown.
They made daisy collars for each
other, too, and pretty daisy cuffs to
go around their paws.

Penny thought that she and
her new friend looked very grand.
"Let's have a princess parade!" she
exclaimed.

"Good idea," cried Bella. "We
can greet all of our loyal subjects!"

Penny scampered across the
meadow, with Bella hopping along

56

behind her. The two princesses waved to a pair of bright orange butterflies that were flitting from flower to flower.

"Good day, beautiful butterflies," Princess Penny shouted in her grandest voice.

"Oh, you sound very royal," Bella whispered, giggling.

They waved to a Dream Deer grazing on the meadow, and a snail inching up a blade of grass.

57

"Greetings, loyal subjects of Honeydew Kingdom," Penny called, while Princess Bella nodded regally to everyone they passed.

They waved to the bees buzzing back to their hive, to the robins building a nest, and to a spider busy spinning a web.

After parading around the whole meadow, Penny and Bella were tired. "These can be our thrones!" Penny panted, flopping

down onto a big rock. Bella sat on a rock next to Penny's.

Perched on their rock thrones, the two pretend princesses looked out over the meadow.

"Honeydew Meadow is the most beautiful kingdom in the world," Penny murmured, and Bella bobbed her head in agreement.

As they rested, they listened to the soothing sounds of the meadow.

Hidden by the long grass, crickets chirped like an orchestra of tiny violins, and birds in the cloudless sky tweeted along. It made Penny want to dance.

"Let's have a royal ball!" exclaimed Penny, leaping off her throne.

She and Bella joined paws and danced around and around to the sweet meadow music. When they were too dizzy to dance anymore,

they collapsed, laughing, in a heap on the grass.

"It's been really fun playing princesses with you, Penny," Bella said when she'd caught her breath. "But now I have to get back to the rabbit warren. I promised my three little brothers that I would tell them a story."

As soon as she heard the word *three*, Penny remembered that it was the last number she had counted.

Oh no! Once again, she'd gotten distracted before she could finish counting. How was she going to be a good Pollen Puppy if she never learned to count to five?

Nuzzling noses with her new friend, and promising to play princesses again soon, Penny hurried off. Playing with Bella had been really fun—but now it was time to get serious about counting!

CHAPTER FOUR

Smooth Sailing

Penny wandered out of Honeydew
Meadow and scratched her ear
thoughtfully. Where could she find
something really, *really* boring to

count? Acorns and daisies had been much too interesting.

Penny gazed around, looking for inspiration . . .

A short distance away, she spied a Bark Badger carving designs on a tree trunk with his sharp claws. Bark Badgers decorated the trunks of the Misty Wood trees with beautiful patterns. They were known to be kind, clever creatures. Penny hoped he might be

able to give her some sound advice.

"Hello," she called, fluttering

over to the Bark Badger. "I'm Penny.

I was wondering if you could help

me—I'm trying to learn how to count."

The badger peered down his long black-and-white snout at Penny. "Why, of course," he said, nodding wisely. "I'm Bobby. And I'm happy to help you—counting is a very important skill for every young fairy animal to learn."

Swiping his claws over the tree's bark, Bobby drew a swirly shape. "One," he said in his deep, rumbly

voice. "Two." As he counted, he drew more whirly shapes on the trunk.

But Penny was struggling to pay attention to the numbers the badger was saying. Instead, her eyes were drawn to the patterns Bobby was making. They reminded her of snail shells. And *this* made her think of how much fun it would be to be a snail.

Imagine carrying your house around on your back! she thought.

Maybe I'll play at being a snail. I could make my very own shell out of tree bark, and . . . Oops!

She'd done it again!

"It's no use," Penny said aloud, shaking her head. "Thank you for trying to help me, Bobby, but your lovely swirly carvings are far too interesting for me to count. I need to find something really boring to practice on."

"Hmm," said Bobby, and

scratched his head. A leaf floated

down from the branches above,

onto the ground in front of them.

Bobby picked it up and handed it

to Penny. "How about leaves?" he suggested. "They aren't *nearly* as interesting as bark."

It was a wonderful idea. "Thank you, Bobby!" Penny exclaimed. Then she dashed off to find more leaves to count.

She collected an oval-shaped leaf from a tall beech tree, a glossy, heart-shaped leaf from a sweet-smelling lilac tree, and a great, big leaf with rough edges from a

chestnut tree. Soon she had more leaves than she could carry, so she laid them all out on the bank of Moonshine Pond.

It's amazing how many different shapes and colors and sizes of leaves there are, thought Penny. But she refused to get distracted by how the leaves looked.

Penny began to count. "One . . . two . . . three . . ."

But when she got to the fourth

leaf, a gust of wind lifted it up into the air. The leaf spun for a moment, twirling on the breeze like a dancer. Then it landed lightly on the shimmering water of Moonshine Pond.

Penny watched as the leaf started to drift across the pond's rippling surface. It was just like a little boat. She thought the leaf looked a bit sad, all alone on the water. It needed some company.

Penny waded into the cool, clear water and floated another leaf on the water's surface. She gave the leaf a gentle push with her nose, and it sailed off on the breeze.

Suddenly, Penny had a brilliant idea. The leaf boats could have a race! She splashed out of the water and gathered up more of her leaves. She set them on the water and watched as they sailed away. At first, an elm leaf was in the

74

lead—but then the big chestnut leaf
quickly gained on it!

One of the leaf boats crashed
into a lily pad and sank under
the surface, and another leaf got

nibbled by a fish, but the rest of Penny's boats sailed proudly across the water.

Penny jumped up and down with excitement, wagging her tail wildly. "Faster! Faster!" she cried, cheering the leaf boats on.

"I'm going as fast as I can," a little voice squeaked.

"Wow! Talking leaf boats!" Penny exclaimed. Even in her wildest daydreams she wouldn't

have imagined
talking leaf boats.

"First you
shout at me to
go faster, then
you call me a talking leaf boat!"
the little voice said crossly.

Penny turned around to see a
tiny brown Moss Mouse down by
the water.

Moss Mice did a very
important job. They shaped velvety

moss into soft cushions so that the fairy animals of Misty Wood would have cozy beds to sleep on.

This Moss Mouse was busy gathering moss from the rocks along the water's edge.

"Oh, dear," Penny said with a laugh, "I wasn't shouting at you— I was cheering my leaf boats on."

"What leaf boats?" the mouse asked. Curious, she scurried over to where Penny stood.

"They're having a race!" Penny explained, pointing at the boats. They were sailing swiftly toward the other side of the pond.

"I wonder which one will win?" murmured the mouse.

"There's only one way to find out," Penny said. "Want to come with me?"

The mouse nodded eagerly. "I'm Marnie," she said.

"Nice to meet you. I'm Penny."

80

Crouching down, she added, "Hop on my back and I'll give you a ride!"

Marnie squeaked excitedly and climbed onto Penny's back. She clung to her fur with tiny paws.

As Penny scampered around the edge of the pond, Marnie told her everything that was happening.

"Ooh! The oak leaf is pulling ahead," Marnie squeaked. "But the elm leaf's close behind."

Running as fast as she could,

Penny let out little yips and yaps
of encouragement to urge the leaf
boats on.

A sudden gust of wind made

all the leaves pick up speed as they skimmed across the pond.

"Now the lilac leaf is in the lead," announced Marnie. "But I wonder, who will make it across first?"

Penny finally got to the other side of the pond and skidded to a stop. Marnie hopped off her back and the two new friends watched the end of the race together.

"We have a winner!" panted

Penny, splashing into the water
to retrieve the lilac leaf.

Padding out of the water, she
shook herself all over, spraying
drops of water everywhere.

Marnie laughed. "Well, when
I came out to do my job today, I
certainly wasn't counting on seeing
a boat race—or getting soaking
wet," she said, brushing shiny drops
of water off her fur.

"Oh no!" Penny groaned as

soon as she heard the word *counting*.
She'd done it *again*. She was meant
to be counting the leaves, not racing
them against one another.

Penny looked up in dismay. The afternoon sun was beginning to dip low in the sky, which glowed with pink and purple streaks. The trees around the pond were casting long shadows across the water's surface.

Penny's heart sank. She'd promised Miss Pammy that she'd learn how to count today—but there was hardly any time left to do it!

CHAPTER FIVE

Sweet Dreams

"What's wrong?" Marnie asked
Penny.

The puppy flopped down on
the ground and covered her eyes

with her paws. "I promised my teacher that I'd learn how to count to five today, but I keep getting distracted. I was supposed to be counting the leaves, but I turned them into boats and now they're gone," she whimpered. "And if I can't count, I'll never be a good Pollen Puppy." Tears glistened in Penny's dark eyes.

"Don't get upset," Marnie said, hopping onto Penny's head and

patting it comfortingly. "I know just the thing for you to count . . ."

Penny took her paws off her eyes and watched hopefully as Marnie scuttled to and fro, her pink tail dragging behind her.

First, the little mouse scurried over to a huge weeping willow tree by the banks of Moonshine Pond. She scooped up piles of moss from around its thick trunk with her nimble paws. Then she darted over

to the damp rocks by the water's edge and gathered up more dark green moss.

Returning to Penny, Marnie patted the moss she'd gathered into five little cushions.

"Ta-da!" she cried, sounding pleased with herself. "Now you can count these!"

Penny ran her paw over the soft, velvety moss cushions. "Thank you so much," she said gratefully.

"But I'm just not sure I have what it takes."

"Don't be silly," Marnie told Penny firmly, dabbing the puppy's tears with a bit of moss. "I *know* you can be a brilliant Pollen Puppy. Just think of how clever you were to come up with the idea for the leaf boat race. Now you just need to focus all of that cleverness on counting."

Penny suddenly felt a lot more

cheerful. Her new friend was so helpful. "Thanks, Marnie."

The Moss Mouse looked up at the orange sky. The moon was just starting to peek out from behind a tree. "I'd better go. I promised my mom I'd be back home before dark. Good luck, Penny. You can do it!"

She kissed Penny on her glossy black nose, then fluttered her sparkly pink wings and rose into the air. As Marnie headed home, Penny

thought she looked like a shooting star, twinkling in the twilight.

Penny glanced down at the moss cushions and remembered what Marnie had told her. She needed to use every bit of cleverness she had to count.

Penny stroked the first moss cushion. "One," she said with determination.

"Two," she said, moving the second cushion alongside the first.

The moss felt so soft and springy. Penny wondered what it would be like to bounce up and down on it . . . up and down and 'round and 'round . . . No! She wasn't going to get distracted—she was going to focus.

"Three," she counted, pushing the third cushion next to the others, and then . . . "Four."

Penny yawned. Counting was so exhausting! Lined up next to one

another, the moss cushions looked like one big, comfy pillow. The sort of pillow that was just the size for a tired Pollen Puppy . . .

It wouldn't hurt to have a little rest, would it? After all, it was very hard to concentrate if you were feeling sleepy.

Penny climbed onto the moss cushion and curled up, tucking her tail beneath her. She let out a little growl of contentment. The moss

was smooth and soft, and even more comfortable than she had imagined. It felt like the cushion was giving her a warm, cozy cuddle!

Penny nestled deeper into the moss. She'd had such a busy day.

Maybe she'd just close her eyes for a moment . . .

Before she knew it, Penny was sound asleep!

As she slept, Penny had an amazing dream. She was having a royal tea party in the Heart of Misty Wood, and all her new friends were there.

"Hello, Princess Penny," called Sammy the Stardust Squirrel, scattering sparkling stardust around

the clearing as he scampered over to her. "I brought you some acorns."

Bella the Bud Bunny hopped over to Penny and nuzzled her nose. "I made this for you, Princess Penny," she said, placing a daisy crown on Penny's head.

Bobby the Bark Badger was busy carving beautiful swirling patterns on the trunks of the oak trees surrounding the clearing.

"It wouldn't be a party without decorations," he said, chuckling.

"We can all sit on these!" Marnie the Moss Mouse cried, shaping soft moss cushions for Penny's guests to sit on.

In her dream, everyone sat down around a tree stump table and nibbled juicy berries, ripe plums, and sweet nuts drizzled with honey.

As Princess Penny and her

friends sipped rosehip tea from acorn caps, a leaf floated down from one of the trees.

"Everyone find a leaf," cried Princess Penny. "We're going to have a boat race!"

In a flash, all the fairy animals were flying through the air to Moonshine Pond. When they landed by the pond, the leaves they were holding grew bigger and bigger and bigger—until they were just the right

size for Penny and her friends to sail on!

"First one to the other side is the winner!" exclaimed Penny, hopping onto a glossy oak leaf.

Penny's silky ears blew back in the breeze as her boat sailed smoothly across the pond. Fluttering her wings as fast as she could, Penny yipped in excitement as her boat took the lead!

But just before she reached the

103

other side of the pond, Penny's leaf

boat suddenly started to shake.

And as the boat started to shake,

Penny started to wobble. And as

she started to wobble, she could feel

herself nearly slide off the leaf—

and into the water! But just before

Penny plunged into the water, she

woke up with a start.

Something—or someone—*was*

shaking her! But it was too dark

to see who it was. The sun had set

long ago and the sky was now an inky black.

Penny's golden fur stood on end. She was afraid of the dark—especially when she was out in it all by herself! Her lovely dream had become a nightmare.

Then she noticed a pale, ghostly light hovering above her. Penny felt even more scared. "Wh-who are you?" she stammered.

CHAPTER SIX

Five New Friends

"Don't be frightened," said a kind
voice. "It's only me—Maisie."

The light moved closer and
Penny realized that it was a net

filled with glowing moonbeams. As it came even nearer, she saw that it was held in the pink claws of a Moonbeam Mole. The mole squinted down her long snout at Penny.

"I was collecting moonbeams and heard you yelping in your sleep," explained Maisie, sounding concerned. "I thought you were having a bad dream, so I woke you up."

"It was actually a wonderful dream, in the beginning," Penny said, her tail drooping. "But I shouldn't have been dreaming at all!" She buried her face in her paws and moaned, "Oh dear, oh

109

dear, oh dear, oh dear, oh dear!"

Marnie chuckled softly. "You just said *oh dear* five times! Can things really be that bad?"

"Yes! And that's just it— everyone can count to five except for me," Penny said, looking up. "I promised my teacher I would learn how today, but instead I had a tea party with my new friend Sammy, played princesses with my new friend Bella, watched my new

friend Bobby draw bark patterns, and had a leaf race with my new friend Marnie. It made me so tired that I fell fast asleep."

Then she wailed, "And I *still* don't know how to count to five!"

"Hmm," Maisie said, drumming her long claws on Penny's moss cushion. "It sounds like you had a lot of fun today."

Penny sniffed. "Yes," she admitted, "I did have lots of fun."

Her tail gave a little twitch of happiness as she thought about her adventures.

"And it sounds like you made a lot of new friends today," Maisie pointed out.

Penny nodded, and her tail started to wag more quickly. "Oh yes," she said, "Sammy, Bella, Bobby, and Marnie were all so nice. I was really lucky to make four new friends in just one day."

Her ears perked up as she realized

what she'd done.

"Oh! I just counted something!"

"Yes, you did," Maisie said

with a smile. "And would you like

to be my friend, too?"

"Of course!" Penny said.

"Well then," Maisie said, tilting her head, "how many friends do you have now?"

Penny's furry brow furrowed as she concentrated hard. "If I have four friends, and I add one more, I have . . ." She looked up at Maisie and smiled more brightly than the mole's net full of moonbeams. "I have five friends!"

"Very good," Maisie exclaimed,

clapping in delight. "So you did learn to count today!"

Penny couldn't wait to show Perry and Miss Pammy and all her friends at school that she'd learned how to count. She would be a good Pollen Puppy after all! Looking up at the luminous moon, Penny let out a little yelp of happiness. But then her yelp turned into a howl.

"Oh no," she groaned. "I may know how to count now, but I don't

know how to find my way home in the dark."

"I'll take you," Maisie offered. "We can use my net of moonbeams to light the way."

"Are you sure?" Penny said. The Moonbeam Moles worked at night, when the other fairy animals were fast asleep. It was their job to gather up moonbeams in their nets and drop them in Moonshine Pond so that the water sparkled and

shimmered. Penny didn't want to get Maisie into trouble.

"Of course," Maisie replied. "That's what friends are for!"

Penny and her newest friend fluttered their wings and rose into the air. They soared over Moonshine Pond, which gleamed in the moonlight. Penny could hear frogs croaking and owls hooting in the distance. High above, stars twinkled like diamonds.

Down below, fireflies danced in the dark like tiny flames.

Penny was surprised to see how beautiful Misty Wood was at night. But then, today had been full of lovely surprises!

Even though she'd come home really late, Penny was so excited that she woke before dawn the next morning. She couldn't wait to get to school! After breakfast, she

bounded into Bluebell Glade and greeted Perry with a cheerful bark.

"Sorry you couldn't come sliding down the rainbow yesterday," Perry said as soon as he saw her. "It was fun. Did you have a really boring afternoon?"

Penny laughed and shook her head. "No, it wasn't boring at all. I made lots of new friends!"

Miss Pammy overheard Penny and joined her students. "Did you

practice your counting as well?" she asked gently.

"I did," Penny said, full of pride. "I made five new friends—Sammy, Bella, Bobby, Marnie, and Maisie."

As she said each of their names, Penny brushed her tail over one bluebell. With each twitch of her tail, a puff of pollen wafted into the air. This time, Penny stopped at five, just as she'd been taught.

She wasn't going to make anyone sneeze ever again!

Perry cheered, and Miss Pammy gave Penny a big hug.

"I'm very impressed," her teacher said. "I knew you could do it!" Then Miss Pammy gave her a playful look.

"If Perry's your friend, too, how many friends do you have in total, Penny?"

Perry started to answer, but

Penny held up her paw to stop him. Perry wasn't the only clever Pollen Puppy now!

"Let me see . . ." she said thoughtfully. "Five plus one more equals . . . six! I have six friends!"

Penny's teacher beamed. "Excellent work! I'm proud of you."

"It was easy," Penny said with a happy bark. "You can always count on your friends!"

Spot the Difference

The picture on the opposite page is slightly different from this one. Can you circle all the differences?

Hint: there are ten
differences in this picture!

Misty Wood Word Search

Can you find all these words from Penny's story?

F	R	I	E	N	D	M	F	L	A	C	O	R	N	I
A	X	E	P	B	L	U	E	B	E	L	L	T	B	N
R	A	I	N	B	O	W	I	B	J	B	E	D	O	V
O	U	Q	S	G	H	Z	A	D	R	E	A	M	A	S
A	P	L	N	C	M	O	S	S	A	N	F	N	T	K

BLUEBELL RAINBOW DREAM LEAF
ACORN MOSS BOAT FRIEND

Connect the Dots

Follow the numbers and connect all the dots to make a lovely picture from the story. Start with dot number 1.

When you've finished connecting the dots, you can color the picture in!

Help Penny
get to her
five bluebells!

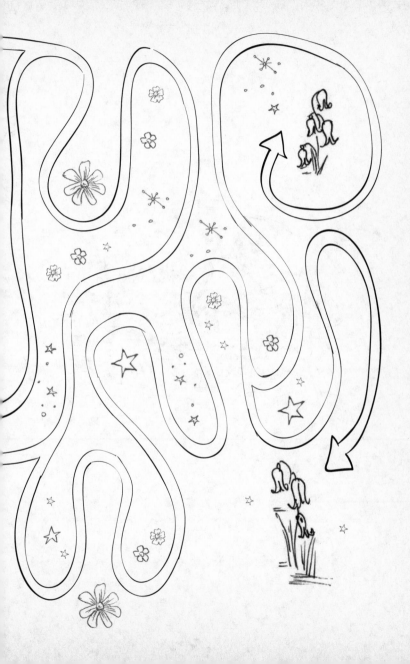